My Weird School Special

We're Red, Weird, and Blue! What Can We Do?

Pictures by
Jim Paillot

Dan Gutman

HARPER
An Imprint of HarperCollinsPublishers

To Emma

ISBN 978-0-06-279684-4 (pbk. bdg.)–ISBN 978-0-06-279685-1 (library bdg.)

Typography by Laura Mock

19 20 21 22 23 PC/LSCH 10 9 8 7 6 5 4 3 2 1

❖

First Edition

Contents

A Hundred Days of Misery

My name is A.J. and I hate February.

February is the shortest month of the year. It's also the worst month of the year. Why, you ask? Four reasons . . .

1. It's cold, rainy, and depressing.

2. The hundredth day of the school year

is in February. A hundred days!* That's a hundred days of *misery*, if you ask me. And we have to *celebrate* it, like going to school for a hundred days is a *good* thing!

3. February is hard to spell because it has an *r* in the middle of it for no reason. What's up with that? It should be spelled Febuary, if you ask me.

But do you want to know the *worst* thing about February?

I'm not gonna tell you.

Okay, okay, I'll tell you.

4. Presidents' Day. Ugh.

Do you know why I hate Presidents' Day? It's a long story. You'd better sit down. If you're already sitting down, stand up.

---

*That's almost a million!

It's all because of what happened *last* Presidents' Day. Or really, what happened just *before* last Presidents' Day, on Crazy Pet Day. My friend Neil brought in his pet ferret, Mr. Wiggles.

That was the day Mr. Macky, our reading specialist, came into our classroom dressed up like Abraham Lincoln. He told us we had to do an oral report about one of the presidents for Presidents' Day. All the students were going to vote for president of the school.

Then our librarian, Mrs. Roopy, came into the classroom dressed like George Washington. She and Mr. Macky told us all about the presidents to help us on our reports, even the weird ones like Millard

Fillmore. Or Fillard Millmore. Or Lardfill Moremill. Whatever his name was.

You're probably wondering what Mr. Wiggles the ferret has to do with Presidents' Day. I'm getting to that.

So anyway, George Washington and Abraham Lincoln started insulting each other. Lincoln said he was better than Washington because he's on the five-dollar bill and Washington is only on the one-dollar bill. Washington said he was better than Lincoln because the Washington Monument is *way* taller than the Lincoln Memorial. The two of them started fighting.

After that, we voted to see which

president would become president of the school. And do you know who won?

I'm not gonna tell you.

Okay, okay, I'll tell you. It wasn't George Washington *or* Abraham Lincoln. The winner was . . . Neil's pet ferret! We all voted for him! Yes, Mr. Wiggles was now *President* Wiggles! That was cool.

After that, we had to give our oral reports. Neil was Thomas Jefferson. Ryan was James Garfield. Michael was Herbert Hoover. In the middle of everything, President Wiggles escaped from his cage and disappeared. Everybody was freaking out. It turned out that President Wiggles was hiding in Abraham Lincoln's hat, which happened to be on Emily's head. That was weird.

I worked really hard on my Presidents' Day oral report. I didn't tell anybody who my president was until the last minute. I wanted it to be a surprise. So I started giving my report about Benjamin Franklin. It was really good. But everybody was looking at me weirdly. Then Little Miss Smarty Pants Andrea Young said, "Benjamin Franklin wasn't a president, dumbhead!"

WHAT?!

It turned out that Andrea was right. Benjamin Franklin was never president of the United States. I just figured that if he was on the hundred-dollar bill, he *had* to be a president. Why else would they put him on the bill? I spent like a million hundred hours learning *everything* about Benjamin Franklin. And for what? Nothing.

It was the worst day of my life. I was totally humiliated in front of the whole school. I wanted to run away to Antarctica and live with the penguins. I thought I was gonna die.

So *that's* why I hate February.

Big Nose

If I was the king of the world, I would change the calendar so it would go straight from January to March. That's right. No more February! But I'm not the king, so of course February came.

We were minding our own business in Mr. Cooper's class. And you'll never believe who ran into the door at that moment.

Nobody! Why would somebody run into a door? That would hurt. But you'll never believe who ran into the door*way*. It was our principal, Mr. Klutz.

"I have big news!" he announced.

"Mr. Klutz has a big nose," I whispered to Michael, who never ties his shoes.

"Next week, we're going to have a contest for all the third graders," said Mr. Klutz.

"Oooooh!" everybody ooooohed, because contests are cool.

"It's going to be Ella Mentry School against Dirk School," said Mr. Klutz.

"Oooooh!" everybody ooooohed again.

Dirk is another school in our town. We call it "Dork School." It's for really smart kids. Ella Mentry and Dirk are big rivals. We competed against them in the Brain Games last year, and we won. It was the greatest day of my life.

"The contest is going to be on the Wednesday right after Presidents' Day," Mr. Klutz told us. "It's going to be called the 'Presidents' Day Challenge.' Doesn't that sound like fun?"

"Yes!" shouted all the girls.

"No!" shouted all the boys.

The Presidents' Day Challenge sounded boring to me. It was sure to be one of those educational snoozefest contests where we have to learn stuff and pretend to be having fun. Learning stuff is no fun.

If we have to learn stuff, why can't we learn about skateboarding or football? Why can't we have a skateboarding contest or a football game against Dirk School? That would be cool.

"Booooooooo!" the guys and me started booing.

"Wait a minute," said Mr. Klutz. "The

wining school will get prizes."

"*Oooooh!*" everybody ooooohed, because winning prizes is cool. And it would be great to beat those Dirk dorks again.

"There will be four prizes," Mr. Klutz told us. "The first prize is bragging rights, of course."

Bragging rights? Who cares? Grown-ups always say you can win bragging rights. But then when we actually brag about something, the grown-ups tell us that bragging isn't nice and we should stop doing it. I'm not falling for *that* again.

"*Booooooooooo!*"

"The second prize is a year's supply of Porky's Pork Sausages," said Mr. Klutz.

I like Porky's Pork Sausages. But every time there's a contest, they give away Porky's Pork Sausages. I bet Mr. Klutz has a secret deal with Peter Porky, the guy who owns the Porky's Pork Sausage company.

"Booooooooo!"

"I think you'll like this," said Mr. Klutz. "The third prize is . . . a trip to DizzyLand."

"Boo—" Wait. WHAT? Did he just say a trip to DizzyLand?

DizzyLand is the coolest place in the history of the world! They've got all kinds of rides there. Some of them not only

make you dizzy, they actually make you throw up. And you know a ride is a good one if it can make you throw up.*

"Yayyyyyyyyyyy!"

Everybody was excited that we could beat those Dirk dorks and win a trip to DizzyLand.

"What's the fourth prize?" asked Andrea, who has to know everything and win everything.

"Oh, the fourth prize is a secret," said Mr. Klutz.

"Ooooooooooh!"

Secrets are cool. Prizes are cool. So secret prizes are supercool.

---

*That's the first rule of throwing up.

Mrs. Roopy Is Loopy!

I didn't think much about the Presidents' Day Challenge until dismissal at three o'clock. The gang and me were about to head home when we saw Andrea and Emily sitting on the front steps of the school. I figured they like school so much, they didn't want to go home.

"What are you doing here?" asked Ryan,

who will eat anything, even stuff that isn't food.

"Emily and I are going to the media center after school today," Andrea said.

"That's right," said Emily, who always agrees with everything Andrea says.

The media center? Ugh. That's a horrible place that used to be called the library, but they changed the name because kids don't want to go to the library. You want to know why? Because it has lots of books in it! Books are boring.*

"Why are you going to the media center?" asked Alexia, who rides a skateboard all the time.

"Mrs. Roopy said she'd help us learn

---

*I don't even know why you're reading this one.

about the presidents," Andrea told us. "The kids who know the most will get to be in the Presidents' Day Challenge."

"So we can win the trip to DizzyLand!" added Emily.

Wait. Only a *few* kids get to go to Dizzy-Land? I thought *all* of us would get to go. It wasn't fair!

Well, I wasn't going to let Andrea win the trip to DizzyLand. When she got up to go to the media center, so did I. And so did Ryan, Neil, Michael, and Alexia. It's not like we had anything better to do after school anyway.

When we got to the media center, our media specialist, Mrs. Roopy, was waiting for us. But she didn't look like Mrs. Roopy.

She's always dressing up like other people. One time she was Little Bo Peep. That was weird. Mrs. Roopy is loopy.

This time, she was dressed up like some old guy, with dark hair and a dark suit and tie.

"Who are you today, Mrs. Roopy?" asked Andrea.

"Roopy?" said Mrs. Roopy in a low voice. "Never heard of her. My name is Ronald Reagan. I was the fortieth president. Before I was the president, I was a movie star. In one movie, my costar was a chimpanzee. The movie was called *Bedtime for Bonzo*."

"So if they ask us which president acted in a movie with a chimp, we'll remember Ronald Reagan," said Andrea.

"See?" said Mrs. Roopy. "You learned something about a president already."

Ronald Roopy Reagan showed us a bunch of books about the presidents. Then he said we could use the computers to look up more stuff. Andrea and Emily rushed to the computer stations.

"I love looking things up online," said Andrea.

"Me too!" said Emily.

"Ooooooh, did you know that four of our presidents were born in February?" asked Andrea. "Washington, Lincoln, Reagan, and William Henry Harrison."

Andrea thinks she is *so* smart because she's a member of P.A.C. That stands for the Principal Advisory Committee—a group of nerds who get to boss around the principal.

Looking up stuff about the presidents was boring. I decided to make an airplane out of the sheet of paper Mrs. Roopy—I mean, Ronald Reagan—gave us. I let it fly, and it almost hit Andrea in the back of her head.

"Arlo!" Andrea yelled. She calls me by my real name because she knows I don't like it. "If you were smart, instead of making paper airplanes, you would be looking to see who was the first president to *fly* in a plane."

"They're never going to ask a dumb question like that," I replied.

"Maybe not," Andrea said. "But you never know when it might come in handy. That's why I'm going to get into Harvard someday. The more I read, the more I know. And the more I know, the smarter I am. And the smarter I am, the more likely I'll go to Harvard and get a good job and be successful in life."

Ugh. Why can't a truck full of Harvards fall on Andrea's head?

"You probably don't know *anything* about the presidents, Arlo," Andrea told me.

"Oh, yeah?" I said. "It just so happens that I know *lots* of stuff about the presidents. I know stuff that nobody else knows."

"Like what?" scoffed Andrea.

"The first flush toilet in the White

House was installed in 1853 by Millard Fillmore," I told her. "I guess before that, the presidents just went in a hole in the ground."

"How do you know that?" everybody asked.

"I also know that George H. W. Bush was the only president to ever throw up on somebody," I said.

"How do you know *that*?" everybody asked.

"I just happen to know a lot of stuff about toilets and puking, okay?" I told them. "It's my jam."

We stayed at the library looking up stuff for a million hundred hours, until our parents came to pick us up. What a snoozefest.

Andrea is sure to win the trip to Dizzy-Land. Her parents hire private tutors to teach her everything. If they had tutors that would teach you how to clip your toenails, Andrea's parents would hire them so Andrea would get better at it.

But I don't think clipping your toenails will get you into Harvard.

A Piece of Cake

The next morning, we were in Mr. Cooper's class.

"Turn to page twenty-three in your math books," he said. That's when an announcement came over the loudspeaker.

"Will the third grade please report to the all-porpoise room?"

"Not again!" groaned Mr. Cooper. "Okay, everybody pringle up."

We all lined up like Pringles and walked a million hundred miles to the all-porpoise room, which should really have a different name because there are no dolphins in there.

Our principal, Mr. Klutz, was waiting for us. He has no hair at all. I mean *none*. He must save a lot of money on haircuts and shampoo. He told us all to climb up on the stage.

"I'm so excited!" Mr. Klutz said. "It's time to choose which of you will represent Ella Mentry School in the Presidents' Day Challenge. Are you kids pumped?"

"Yes!" shouted all the girls.

"No!" shouted all the boys.

"I'm going to ask you questions about the presidents," Mr. Klutz explained. "Blah blah blah blah. Whoever gets the most right will compete against Dirk School next week blah blah blah blah."

Annoying Andrea was sitting in front of me. I heard her whisper to Emily.

"I'm in the gifted and talented program," Andrea whispered. "This is going to be a piece of cake."

What does cake have to do with any-thing?

Andrea got the first question, of course.

"Which president said 'it is easier to do a job right than to explain why you didn't'?" asked Mr. Klutz.

I had no idea.

"The answer is Martin Van Buren," Andrea said. "He was the eighth president of the United States."

"That's right!" said Mr. Klutz. "Very good, Andrea. I can see you've been studying."

Andrea smiled the smile she smiles to let everybody know she knows something nobody else knows. What is her problem?

"Okay, A.J., it's your turn," said Mr. Klutz.

"This is a tough one. Who was president when the first flush toilet was installed in the White House?"

I knew that!

"Millard Fillmore!" I shouted.

"That's right!" said Mr. Klutz. "Very good, A.J. I see you've been studying too."

I stuck my tongue out at Andrea. Next it was Ryan's turn.

"Who was the third president of the United States?" asked Mr. Klutz.

"John Adams?" guessed Ryan.

"Incorrect," said Mr. Klutz. "Sorry, Ryan. Adams was the *second* president. The third president was Thomas Jefferson. Nice try, though."

Ryan walked off the stage and took a

seat in the front row. Next, it was Michael's turn.

"Who was president when the Civil War started?" asked Mr. Klutz.

"Andrew Jackson?" guessed Michael.

"No, that's not it," said Mr. Klutz. "Sorry, Michael. The correct answer is Abraham Lincoln."

Michael walked off the stage. It was Neil's turn.

"Which president said 'the only thing we have to fear is fear itself'?" asked Mr. Klutz.

"John F. Kennedy?" guessed Neil.

"Nice try, but no," said Mr. Klutz. "Sorry, Neil. The correct answer is Franklin Delano Roosevelt."

Neil walked off the stage. It was Emily's turn.

"Emily, what does L.B.J. stand for?"

"Lyndon...Bobby...Johnson?" guessed Emily.

"Close," said Mr. Klutz. "Sorry, Emily. The correct answer is Lyndon *Baines* Johnson."*

Emily walked off the stage. It was Alexia's turn.

"Seven of our first twelve presidents were born in what state?" asked Mr. Klutz.

"Uh...Massachusetts?" guessed Alexia.

"Nope," said Mr. Klutz. "Sorry, Alexia. The correct answer is Virginia."

Alexia walked off the stage. One by one,

---

*Baines?! That's a weird name.

everybody was getting eliminated. Finally, it was just me and Andrea on the stage.

"Okay, now it's down to two students," said Mr. Klutz.

I looked at Andrea. She stuck her tongue out at me. I stuck my tongue out at her. When you don't like somebody, you should always stick your tongue out at them. Nobody knows why. But it's the first rule of being a kid.

"Andrea," asked Mr. Klutz, "what was

George Washington's wife's name?"

"Martha!" Andrea replied right away.

"That's right!" said Mr. Klutz. "A.J., which president once threw up on a foreign dignitary?"

"George H. W. Bush!" I shouted.

"That's right!" said Mr. Klutz. "And for a bonus point, who did he throw up on?"

"The prime minister of Japan!" I shouted.

"Very good, A.J.," said Mr. Klutz.

I stuck my tongue out at Andrea again. As long as Mr. Klutz kept asking questions about toilets and presidents who threw up on people, I would be fine.

"Andrea," said Mr. Klutz, "which president's first name at birth was Leslie?"

Wow. These questions were *tough*.

"Gerald Ford!" Andrea shouted.

"Right!" said Mr. Klutz. "It's going to be hard to choose between you two. A.J., who was the president from 1929 to 1933?"

Uh-oh. I didn't know that one. I was going to lose. Andrea would be competing against Dirk School in the Presidents' Day Challenge, and she would be going to DizzyLand.

"Uh . . ." I tried to think of who was the president from 1929 to 1933.

In the front row, Michael caught my eye. He was making weird hand motions. It almost looked like he was vacuuming a floor. That was weird.

"Michael, what are you doing?" asked Mr. Klutz.

"I'm, uh . . . pretending to use a vacuum cleaner," Michael replied.

Vacuum cleaner?

"Hoover!" I shouted. "The correct answer is Hoover!"

"That's right!" said Mr. Klutz. "Very good, A.J.! Andrea, which president has the same first name as a character on *Sesame Street*?"

"Grover Cleveland!" shouted Andrea.

"Right!" said Mr. Klutz. "A.J., who was the fourth president?"

I had no idea. This was it. I was finished. In the front row, Ryan was making hand motions. He looked like he was arguing with somebody.

"Ryan, what are you doing?" asked Mr. Klutz.

"Uh . . . nothing," Ryan replied. "I'm just pretending to be a guy who's mad at his son."

Mad at his son?

"Madison!" I shouted. "The correct answer is Madison!"

"That's right!" said Mr. Klutz. "Very good, A.J.!"

"That's not fair!" Andrea shouted. "Arlo's friends are feeding him the answers. He's cheating!"

"I am not," I shouted.

"Are too," shouted Andrea.

"R2D2," I shouted.

We went back and forth like that for a while.

Mr. Klutz had to make the shut-up

peace sign with his fingers to calm everybody down.

"I can select two third graders," he said. "I think it's obvious which of our students know the most about the presidents. Andrea and A.J. will *both* represent our school at the Presidents' Day Challenge."

Everybody clapped their hands in a circle to give us a round of applause.

"Oooooh," said Ryan. "A.J. and Andrea will be in the Presidents' Day Challenge *together.* They must be in *love!*"

"When are you gonna get married?" asked Michael.

If those guys weren't my best friends, I would hate them.

I Quit!

So Andrea and I would be representing our school. Ugh. I didn't want to do it. I might actually have to learn something about the presidents. What a waste! The more time you spend learning stuff, the less time you have to spend on important stuff, like watching TV and playing video games.

But everybody at school was really getting into it. All the kids wanted to see us beat those Dirk School dorks again. All the teachers were feeding Andrea and me facts about the presidents to help us get ready.

When we went to the media center, Mrs. Roopy showed us more books and videos about the presidents.

During computer class, our computer teacher, Mrs. Yonkers, told us that Bill Clinton was the first president to use email.

During music class, our music teacher, Mr. Loring, told us that Bill Clinton also played the saxophone on TV.

During fizz ed, our gym teacher, Miss

Small, told us that Gerald Ford was a star football player when he was in college at the University of Michigan.

All the grown-ups at school kept pulling Andrea and me aside in the hallway to tell us facts they knew about the presidents. Our security guard, Officer Spence, told me about how the Secret Service protects the president. He said you never know what questions might be asked at the Presidents' Day Challenge.

Even Coach Hyatt, my Pee Wee football coach, wanted to help.

"A.J.," she shouted to me at the end of practice on Saturday. "I want you and Andrea to pick up my car."

"What?!" I replied. "How would picking

up your car help us win the Presidents'
Day Challenge?"

"Pick it up!" she shouted back. "Show us
how tough you are. If you can pick up a
car, you can do anything."

That was weird. Coach Hyatt is a riot.

Finally, it was Presidents' Day. We had that
day off from school, and the Presidents'
Day Challenge would be on Wednesday
night. On Tuesday morning, we were in
Mr. Cooper's class when an announcement came over the loudspeaker.

"Andrea and A.J., please report to Mr.
Klutz's office."

Uh-oh.

"Oooooh," said Ryan. "A.J. and Andrea

are going to Mr. Klutz's office together. They must be in *love*!"

"When are you gonna get married?" asked Michael.

Andrea and I walked a million hundred miles to Mr. Klutz's office. When we got there, he was hanging upside down from the ceiling.

"Why are you hanging upside down from the ceiling?" Andrea asked.

"It helps me think," Mr. Klutz replied. "Your brain works better after the blood has rushed to your head. You should try it."

Mr. Klutz is nuts. He climbed down and sat behind his desk.

"Did we do something wrong?" I asked. Usually, I get called to the principal's office when I did something wrong.

"No, no, no," Mr. Klutz replied. "Just the opposite. I'm so proud of you two. Win or lose, you'll be representing our school. You're going to be under a lot of pressure tomorrow night. The questions will be harder. There may be some trick questions too. I know you're both going to give it your best shot."

I looked at Andrea. She had on her mean face.

"What's the matter, Andrea?" asked Mr. Klutz.

"Arlo doesn't know *anything* about the presidents," she complained. "He's not prepared, and he's not even trying."

"I know *lots* of stuff about the presidents!" I said.

"Oh, yeah," Andrea said. "You know which president put a toilet in the White House. You know which president threw up on somebody. But that's *all* you know. Arlo is going to bring our team down, Mr. Klutz."

"Hey, I didn't want to do this in the first place," I shouted. "I don't want everybody to think I'm some kind of brainiac like *you*. All my friends are making fun of me. You know what? I quit! Do it yourself."

I went to open the door, but Mr. Klutz stood up and blocked me. He came and put his arms around me and Andrea.

"Look," he said gently. "You two kids have known each other for a long time.

You were chosen to represent Ella Mentry School because you're really smart. You're both in the gifted and talented program. I need you to put aside your differences and work together as a team for the good of the school. Can you do that for one night?"

"Okay," Andrea and I replied softly.

We walked a million hundred miles back to our classroom without saying anything. But Andrea seemed to cheer up just as we got to the door.

"I have an idea, Arlo!" she said excitedly. "Why don't you come over to my house after school today. We can be study buddies!"

Study buddies? I didn't want to be

Andrea's study buddy! I just hoped my friends didn't hear her say that as we walked into the classroom.

"Oooooh," said Ryan. "A.J. and Andrea are going to be study buddies. They must be in *love*!"

"When are you gonna get married?" asked Michael.*

---

*If you think we've overdone that joke, send your angry emails to idontcare@leavemealone.please.

The Presidents' Day Challenge

Finally, it was the big night. My mom made me get all dressed up in a jacket and tie. Ugh.

"You look so handsome!" she told me.

I felt like I was going to a funeral. My own. As we drove to school, I started thinking—I don't know *anything* about the presidents. Why do I have to represent the school?

When we got to the all-porpoise room, the place was packed. All my friends and classmates were there, along with lots of kids and parents from Dirk School. Some of the kids were holding signs. Some were chanting.

"Dirk! Dirk! Dirk!"

There was electricity in the air.

Well, not really. If there was electricity in the air, all of us would have been electrocuted.

But everybody who was *anybody* was there. Dr. Carbles, the president of the board of education, was in the front row. So was Peter Porky, the owner of Porky's Pork Sausages. He was sitting between Mayor Hubble and Mr. Wilson, the principal of Dirk School. Even Ella Mentry, the old lady our school was named after, was there.

My parents wished me good luck and took the only seats that were left, in the back of the room. I walked down the middle aisle to get to the front. Lots of people took pictures and held out their hands for me to slap.

"We're counting on you, A.J.!"

"Don't let us down, A.J.!"

"No pressure, A.J.!"

"If we lose, it will be all your fault, A.J.!"

"Just have fun, A.J.!"

"You'd better win, A.J.!"

I took a seat next to Andrea in the front row.

"It's about time you showed up, Arlo," Andrea whispered. "I thought you were going to chicken out."

"No way," I replied. "I'm in it to win it."

Mr. Peter Porky of Porky's Pork Sausages

climbed up on the stage. Everybody clapped.

"Welcome, boys and girls, parents, teachers, and all our guests," said Mr. Porky. "I will be the moderator of tonight's Presidents' Day Challenge and blah blah blah blah . . ."

He went on for a million hundred min-

Mostly, he talked about :ky's Pork Sausages.

". . . and now I'd like to introduce the home team," Mr. Porky said. "From Ella Mentry School . . . two third graders in the gifted

and talented program . . . A.J. and Andrea!"

"Ella Mentry! Ella Mentry! Ella Mentry!" our classmates chanted as we climbed on the stage and took seats at one of the two tables up there.

"Dirk! Dirk! Dirk!" chanted the Dirk kids.

"And from the visiting team at Dirk School," said Mr. Porky, "I'd like to introduce two exceptional third graders . . . Tommy and Morgan!"

Oh no, not Morgan Brocklebank! She's the star of the Dirk School TV station. We competed against her in the Brain Games.* She is annoying.

---

*You can read about it in *Miss Brown Is Upside Down!*

Morgan and Tommy climbed up onstage and took seats at the table next to us. The whole audience stood up and gave us a round of applause.

"Well, well, well," Morgan Brocklebank said to me while everybody was clapping. "We meet again. Are you two ready to *lose*?"

"Your *face* is gonna lose!" I said, pointing my finger at her.

"Oh, yeah?" Morgan Brocklebank replied. "I don't *think* so. Tommy and I went to Washington to do research on the presidents. We know *everything*. I hope you two will have something to do while we're having fun at DizzyLand."

"You're going to *Loser*Land!" I told her.

Meanwhile, that kid Tommy just sat there, picking his nose.

"We're going to *crush* you!" said Morgan Brocklebank. "This is going to be a cakewalk."

What did cake have to do with it? Why is everybody always talking about cake?

Finally, the audience sat down in their

seats. It was time to start the Presidents' Day Challenge.

I was nervous. Suddenly, I felt my mind going blank. I forgot everything I learned over the last week. Who was the first president? I couldn't remember his name. I only remembered that it had something to do with laundry. George Detergenton? I was all sweaty.

I thought I was gonna die.

Round One

"Let's go over the rules," said Mr. Porky. "I will ask each team a question blah blah blah blah ten seconds to answer blah blah blah blah one point for each correct answer blah blah blah blah then a lightning round blah blah blah blah and one final question for both teams blah blah blah blah. There may be a few trick questions in there too, so stay on your toes."

Why should we stay on our toes? That made no sense at all. I was going to sit on a chair like everybody else.

"Before we begin round one," continued Mr. Porky, "please join me in singing the Porky's Pork Sausage jingle."

Two fifth graders from our school orchestra came up on the stage with violins. They played while Peter Porky sang . . .

Porky's Pork Sausages
The best sausages in the land.
Porky's Pork Sausages
You can eat them with your hands

What a dumb song.

"I don't approve of these violins," I whispered to Andrea.

"Quiet, Arlo."

I looked over at that doofus Tommy. He was still picking his nose.

"Okay, let's get started with round one," said Mr. Porky, reaching into his pocket. "I'll flip a coin to see which school goes first. Call it!"

"Heads!" I shouted as Mr. Porky flipped the coin.

"Heads, it is," said Mr. Porky. "Ella Mentry School gets the first question. Is everybody ready?"

"Ready!" Andrea and I shouted.

"Ready!" Morgan and Tommy shouted.

"Okay," said Mr. Porky. "Which president had a pet raccoon that would roam around the White House?"

What? I didn't know that. Why would *anybody*

know that? I looked at Andrea. She shrugged her shoulders.

"I'll give you a hint," said Mr. Porky. "The raccoon's name was Rebecca."

"Calvin Coolidge!" shouted Andrea.

"That's right!" said Mr. Porky. "One point for the Ella Mentry team."

Everybody cheered. Andrea smiled the smile that she smiles to let everybody know she knows something nobody else knows. I leaned over to her.

"Wait a second," I whispered. "You didn't know which president had a raccoon, but you knew the name of the raccoon?"

"Yes!" Andrea whispered back.

That was weird.

"The next question is for Dirk School,"

said Mr. Porky. "Name two presidents who signed the Declaration of Independence."

Morgan and Tommy whispered to each other for a few seconds.

"John Adams and Thomas Jefferson," Morgan said.

"Correct!" said Mr. Porky. "The score is one to one."

Wow. Those Dirk dorks are *smart*.

"The next question is for Ella Mentry," said Mr. Porky. "Fifty-seven people signed the Declaration of Independence. How many of them were women?"

I had no idea.

"It's a trick question!" Andrea shouted. "*None* of them were women! And it's not fair!"

"Right!" shouted Mr. Porky. "Very good, Andrea. The score is two to one. The next question is for Dirk. Name two presidents who signed the Constitution."

Morgan and Tommy whispered to each other.

"George Washington and James Madison," shouted Morgan.

"Correct!" said Mr. Porky. "It's all tied up at two to two. Isn't this exciting? Ella Mentry, which president grew up on a peanut farm?"

I had no idea.

"Jimmy Carter!" shouted Andrea. She is really smart.

"Right!" said Mr. Porky. "Three to two now. Dirk, who was the first president to ride in an airplane?"

"See?" Andrea whispered in my ear. "I told you they might ask that question."

"Teddy Roosevelt!" shouted Morgan Brocklebank.

"That's right!" said Mr. Porky. "It's now tied at three to three. Ella Mentry, Thomas Jefferson and John Adams did *not* sign the Constitution. Why not?"

I had no idea. I looked over at Andrea.

"What are you looking at me for?" she whispered.

"I thought you knew everything," I whispered back.

"Well, I *don't*! It would help if you knew *anything*!"

"Maybe those guys were in the bathroom when the other guys were signing the Constitution," I whispered.

"Don't you *dare* say that, Arlo!" Andrea whispered.

A buzzer rang.

"Time's up," said Mr. Porky. "They didn't sign the Constitution because they were overseas at the time! Thomas Jefferson was representing the United States in France, and John Adams was doing the same thing in England."

"Ohhhhhhh," the audience groaned.

"I should have known that!" Andrea said, slamming her fist against the table.

"It's still tied up at three points each,"

said Mr. Porky. "Dirk School, who was the first president to have electricity in the White House?"

"Benjamin Harrison!" shouted Morgan Brocklebank.

"Correct!" said Mr. Porky. "The score is now four to three in favor of Dirk. Ella Mentry, you can tie it up again. Only one of our presidents was born on the Fourth of July. Who was it?"

I had no idea. Andrea didn't look very sure of herself.

"Grover Cleveland?" she finally answered.

"No, sorry," said Mr. Porky. "The correct answer is Calvin Coolidge."

"Ohhhhhhh," the audience groaned.

That was the end of round one. Dirk was leading, four to three. Andrea looked mad. But there was still plenty of time for us to catch up.

Round Two

"Okay," said Mr. Porky. "Round two will be the lightning round."

"We're going to get struck by lightning?" I asked. Everybody laughed even though I didn't say anything funny. Andrea rolled her eyes and slapped her own forehead.

"This is going to go fast," said Mr. Porky. "You only get five seconds to answer each question, and each question is worth two points. I'll tally up the points at the end."

Andrea leaned over to me.

"Arlo, you've got to get your act together!" she whispered. "You haven't answered *any* questions."

"Chillax," I replied.

"Okay, Ella Mentry School started round one," said Mr. Porky, "so Dirk School will start round two. Ready?"

"Ready!" Morgan shouted. Tommy picked his nose.

"Name a president who won a Grammy Award," said Mr. Porky.

"Bill Clinton!" shouted Morgan.

"Right!" said Mr. Porky. "Ella Mentry, which president proclaimed the first Thanksgiving?"

"George Washington!" shouted Andrea.

"Right!" said Mr. Porky. "Which president worked at Baskin-Robbins and collected Spider-Man comics?"

"Barack Obama!" shouted Morgan.

"Right!" said Mr. Porky. "Who was the first president to live in the White House?"

"John Adams!" shouted Andrea.

"Right!" said Mr. Porky. "Whose face is on the five-thousand-dollar bill?"

There's a five-thousand-dollar bill?*

"James Madison!" shouted Morgan.

"Right!" said Mr. Porky. "Besides Presidents' Day, what other holidays fall in February?" asked Mr. Porky.

"Super Bowl Sunday!" I shouted. Everybody laughed even though I didn't say anything funny.

"I'll give that one to you," said Mr. Porky. "I was thinking of Valentine's Day and Groundhog Day. Dirk, who was the shortest president?"

---

*It must be tough to get change for that. "I'd like to buy a pack of gum. Can you change a five-thousand-dollar bill?"

"James Madison!" shouted Morgan.

"Right!" said Mr. Porky. "He was only five feet four inches tall. Ella Mentry, which president was shot a year before Abraham Lincoln?"

I looked at Andrea. She shrugged her shoulders.

"Uh . . . it was . . . "

"Time's up," said Mr. Porky. "It was Abraham Lincoln. Another trick question. He was riding a horse when a shot rang out. It didn't hit him, but the bullet hole went through his hat."

"I knew that!" Andrea said, pounding the table.

"Dirk School," said Mr. Porky. "When Washington became president, how many real teeth were in his mouth?"

"One!" shouted Morgan.

"Right!" said Mr. Porky. "Which president had grizzly bear cubs that lived in a cage on the White House lawn?"

"Thomas Jefferson!" shouted Andrea.

"Right!" said Mr. Porky. "What treat did James Madison's wife, Dolley, serve at his inauguration ball?"

"Ice cream!" shouted Morgan.

"Right!" said Mr. Porky. "Which president had a bullet in his shoulder for most of his life?"

"James Monroe!" shouted Andrea. "He was shot during the Revolutionary War."

"Right!" said Mr. Porky. "Name three presidents who died on the Fourth of July."

"John Adams, Thomas Jefferson, and James Monroe!" shouted Morgan.

"Right!" said Mr. Porky.

"WOW," I said, which is "MOM" upside

down. I had lost track of the score, but Morgan and Andrea *really* knew their stuff. I was pretty much useless to our team, and Tommy just sat there picking his nose. Mr. Porky continued.

"Which president used to go swimming naked in the Potomac River?"

"John Quincy Adams!" shouted Andrea.

"Right!" said Mr. Porky. "Which president was only president for a month?"

"William Henry Harrison!" shouted Morgan.

"Right!" said Mr. Porky. "Which president had the most children?"

"John Tyler!" shouted Andrea.

"Right!" said Mr. Porky. "How many

children did John Tyler have?"

"Fifteen!" shouted Morgan.

"Right!" said Mr. Porky. "Where did Abraham Lincoln store his mail, his bankbook, and important papers?"

"In his hat!" shouted Andrea.

"Right!" said Mr. Porky. "Who was the first president to have a telephone in the White House?"

"Rutherford B. Hayes!" shouted Morgan.

"Right!" said Mr. Porky. "Who installed Rutherford B. Hayes's telephone?"

"Alexander Graham Bell, the inventor of the telephone!" shouted Andrea.

"Right!" said Mr. Porky. "What was Rutherford B. Hayes's phone number?"

"It was *one*!" shouted Morgan.

"Right!" said Mr. Porky. "Which president owned eighty pairs of pants?"

"Chester A. Arthur!" shouted Andrea.

"Right!" said Mr. Porky. "Who was the first president to ride in a car?"

"William McKinley!" shouted Morgan.

"Right!" said Mr. Porky. "Which president is responsible for the invention of the teddy bear?"

"Teddy Roosevelt!" shouted Andrea.

"Right!" said Mr. Porky. "Which president, legend has it, got stuck in a White House bathtub?"

"William Taft!" shouted Morgan. "He weighed over three hundred pounds."

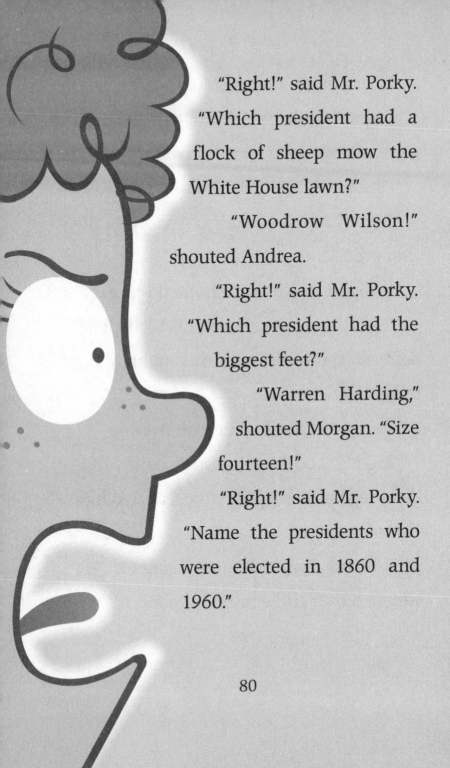

"Right!" said Mr. Porky. "Which president had a flock of sheep mow the White House lawn?"

"Woodrow Wilson!" shouted Andrea.

"Right!" said Mr. Porky. "Which president had the biggest feet?"

"Warren Harding," shouted Morgan. "Size fourteen!"

"Right!" said Mr. Porky. "Name the presidents who were elected in 1860 and 1960."

"Lincoln and Kennedy!" shouted Andrea.

"Right!" said Mr. Porky. "Which president had a secretary named Kennedy?"

"Lincoln!" shouted Morgan.

"Right!" said Mr. Porky. "Which president had a secretary named Lincoln?"

"Kennedy!" shouted Andrea.

"Right!" said Mr. Porky. "Name the two presidents who had vice presidents named Johnson."

That would be "Lincoln and Kennedy!" shouted Morgan.

"Right!" said Mr. Porky. "Doesn't that take the cake?"

What did cake have to do with anything? Why is everybody always talking about cake?

"Which president had a bowling alley installed in the White House?"

"Harry S. Truman!" shouted Andrea.

"Right!" said Mr. Porky. "Which president worked as a fashion model and appeared on the cover of *Cosmopolitan* magazine?"

"Gerald Ford!" shouted Morgan.

"Right!" said Mr. Porky. "And who makes

the best pork sausages?"

"Porky's!" we all shouted.

"Right!" said Mr. Porky. "Okay, that's the end of round two. Whew! That was intense! Let's all take a deep breath, and then I'll tally up the points."

The audience clapped and cheered for a million hundred seconds. Finally, Mr. Porky looked up from his score sheet.

"The scores are . . . Dirk School thirty-eight points and Ella Mentry School thirty-three points. Dirk has a five-point lead going into the final round."

All the Dirk kids started hooting and hollering. Morgan Brocklebank sneered at me and made the L sign with her fingers.

Andrea looked really mad.

"We're losing," she said to me. "And it's all because of you, Arlo! Don't you know *anything*? I can't carry the team all by myself."

I wanted to say something mean to Andrea, but how could I? She was right. I didn't know anything. We were getting crushed, and it was my fault.

I wanted to go run away to Antarctica and live with the penguins. Penguins don't have to know about the presidents. I'm not even sure if Antarctica *has* a president.

This was the worst day of my life.

All the Marbles

"Okay, it all comes down to round three," announced Mr. Porky. "This last question is for *both* teams. Write your answer on the sheet of paper in front of you. It's worth *six* points."

"Ooooooh!" everybody oooooohed.

"Dirk has a five-point lead," continued Mr. Porky. "So if both teams get this question right, Dirk wins. If both teams get it wrong, Dirk also wins. If Dirk gets it right and Ella Mentry gets it wrong, Dirk still wins. But if Dirk gets it wrong and Ella Mentry gets it right, Ella Mentry wins. Does everybody understand?"

"Yes," I lied.

"We *have* to get this one right, Arlo," Andrea whispered to me.

"Okay," said Mr. Porky. "This one is for all the marbles."

Marbles? What did marbles have to do with anything?

"Get ready to lose, losers!" said Morgan Brocklebank, rubbing her hands together. "This will be the icing on the cake."

Why is everybody always talking about

marbles and cake? Was the winning team going to get marble cake? I was confused.

In the audience, nobody was making a sound. It was so quiet, you could hear a pin drop. That is, if anybody had brought pins with them. That would be weird. But everybody was on the edge of their seats.

Well, not really. There might have been a few little kids on the edge of their seats, but most normal-size people were just sitting in the middle of their seats.

Anyway, it was really tense. Andrea picked up our pencil and got ready to write the answer.

"Okay, here's your final question," said Mr. Porky. "And before I give it to you, let me just say that Porky's Pork Sausages will be on sale at your local supermarket next week."

Everybody laughed even though he didn't say anything funny.

"Okay, here's the final question," said Mr. Porky, reading from a card. "My birthday was January seventeenth. My wife was named Deborah. I played the violin, the harp, and the guitar. I was a slave owner. I died when I was eighty-four years old. Who am I? You have thirty seconds."

That annoying music from the TV show *Jeopardy!* started playing.* I looked at Andrea.

---

*Ask your mom or dad if you can YouTube it. Or watch the TV show.

"Do you know who it is?" I asked.

"No," she replied. "Do you?"

"No."

"Of course you don't," Andrea said. "You didn't know *any* of the answers."

I looked over at the Dirk dorks. They were whispering to each other.

"Twenty seconds left," said Mr. Porky.

"*You're* the smart one," I whispered to Andrea. "You memorized the encyclopedia. You keep a dictionary on your desk at school. Your parents got a tutor to teach you all about the presidents. How can you not know the answer?"

"I just don't, okay?" Andrea whispered back angrily. "*You're* part of this team too, you know. You were supposed to help, Arlo. Maybe if you weren't making paper airplanes and goofing off all week, you would know the answer!"

"Fifteen seconds left," said Mr. Porky. The dumb *Jeopardy!* song was still playing.

"Why are we wasting time arguing?" I whispered to Andrea. "We should be trying to come up with the answer."

I saw Morgan Brocklebank write something on her paper. She and Tommy probably knew the answer. They were going to win. We had nothing.

"Ten seconds left," said Mr. Porky.

"Any ideas?" I whispered to Andrea.

"No!" she replied angrily. "Just write down *any* president, Arlo. I don't care anymore. We lost. It's over. Thanks for nothing!"

Andrea looked like she was going to cry. I had never seen her like that. She always wins at *everything*.

"Five seconds left," said Mr. Porky.

I didn't know what to say. I didn't know

what to do. I had to think fast. I was concentrating so hard that my brain hurt.

That's when I got the greatest idea in the history of the world.

But I'm not going to tell you what it was.

Okay, okay, I'll tell you. But you have to read the next chapter.

The Big Surprise Ending

I grabbed the pencil out of Andrea's hand and quickly wrote my answer on the paper. That dumb *Jeopardy!* song ended.

"Okay, pencils down," said Mr. Porky. "Dirk, you go first. I'll repeat the question. My birthday was January seventeenth. My wife was named Deborah. I played the violin, the harp, and the guitar. I was a slave owner. I died when I was eighty-four years old. Who am I?"

Morgan Brocklebank held up her piece of paper. It said ANDREW JOHNSON on it.

"No, sorry," said Mr. Porky. "That is incorrect."

"*Ohhhhhhhh,*" groaned the Dirk half of the audience. Morgan pounded the table with her fist.

"Dirk still wins if the Ella Mentry team gets it wrong," said Mr. Porky. "Ella Mentry, what is your answer?"

Everybody in the audience was glued to their seats. Well, not really. That would be weird. Why would anybody glue themselves to a seat? How would they get the glue off their pants?

But everyone was looking at me. I held up my piece of paper. It said BENJAMIN FRANKLIN on it.

"Benjamin Franklin wasn't a president, dumbhead!" Andrea yelled at me. She was furious. "I can't believe it! How could you make that same mistake *again*?"

"BENJAMIN FRANKLIN IS CORRECT!" shouted Mr. Porky. "It was a trick question! I never said the person was a president! Ella Mentry School is the winner!"

Everybody in the all-porpoise room started yelling and screaming and hooting and hollering and freaking out. All my friends rushed up onstage to give me high fives. Andrea said she was sorry for calling me a dumbhead. It was the greatest moment of my life.*

I looked over at Morgan Brocklebank. She was furious.

"We only studied the presidents!" she

---

*I should get the Nobel Prize. That's a prize they give out to people who don't have bells.

shouted. "It's not fair!"

She looked like she was going to cry. I almost felt sorry for her. I went over to her and said these five immortal words . . .

"Nah-nah-nah boo-boo!"

DizzyLand

The Presidents' Day Challenge was such a success that our whole class got to go to DizzyLand. We went on all the rides. I almost threw up three or four times. It was awesome.

One of the coolest parts of DizzyLand is the Wall of Presidents. It's an exhibit with life-size statues of all the presidents. The coolest part is that they're robots. So they can nod their heads, wave their hands, and even give speeches. The president robots look really real.

The Abraham Lincoln robot was giving his speech when the weirdest thing in the history of the world happened. Lincoln is Emily's favorite president, and I guess she got a little too close to him, because the statue started to topple over. It fell against President Truman. Truman bumped into President Nixon, and Nixon knocked over President Grant.

The next thing we knew, the rest of the presidents were going down like

dominoes. We got to see it live and in person. You should have been there!

"Watch out!" shouted Alexia.

"Help! The presidents are attacking!" shouted Ryan.

"Run for your lives!" shouted Neil.

In the end, the president robot statues were all over the floor and we had to crawl out from under them. That was weird.

Well, that's pretty much what happened. Maybe Millard Fillmore will flush his toilet. Maybe grown-ups will stop saying blah blah blah blah all the time. Maybe President Bush will stop throwing up on people. Maybe Porky's Pork Sausages will get a new jingle. Maybe President Obama will go back to scooping ice cream at Baskin-Robbins. Maybe President Taft will go on Weight Watchers. Maybe next year we'll figure out a way to knock February off the calendar.

But it won't be easy!

Oh, I almost forgot! We got *another* prize for winning the Presidents' Day Challenge. Besides bragging rights, a year's supply of Porky's Pork Sausages, and the trip to DizzyLand, there was that secret prize.

But I'm not going to tell you what it was.

Okay, okay, I'll tell you.

It was cake.*

---

*I guess that's why everybody was always talking about cake.

MY WeiRd School SpeciaL

We're Red, Weird, and Blue! What Can We Do?

WEIRD EXTRAS!

★ Professor Andrea's Presidents' Day Facts

★ Fun Games and Weird Word Puzzles

★ My Weird School Trivia Questions

★ The World of Dan Gutman Checklist

PROFESSOR ANDREA'S PRESIDENTS' DAY FACTS

Hi, everybody! Andrea here.

Arlo really helped us win the Presidents' Day Challenge, but he got lucky. The truth is that he doesn't know *anything* about the presidents. Or about anything else.

Me, I know *lots* of stuff. I'm going to Harvard when I'm older. So I thought I'd take this opportunity to teach you how to learn new stuff. It's easy and it's fun too.

Let's say you want to learn more about the presidents, or any other subject. The first place you should go is your local public library. If you don't know where it is, the library is that big building in the center of town that says PUBLIC LIBRARY on the front. Duh! Some of the older ones even say PVBLIC LIBRARY. Arlo would say nobody knows why. But I looked it up. In Latin, the letter that is our *V* was used for the *U* sound. Isn't that interesting?

Anyway, once you're in the library, go to the nonfiction section and look for number 923.1. That's part of the Dewey decimal system. A number will be on the spine of all the nonfiction books. Every library uses this system, and every topic in the world has its own number. When you get to 923.1, you're going to see books about the presidents.

Well, that is unless somebody like me checked them all out already. But you should be able to put a book on reserve. The librarian can help you with that. Librarians are really nice people who know lots of things. Maybe I'll be a librarian after I graduate from Harvard.

Let's say the president books in your public library are all checked out, or your public library is really far away. Is there a bookstore nearby? They don't organize the shelves by the Dewey decimal system, but they probably have books about the presidents too. If you can't find them on the shelf, ask somebody in the children's department. They should be able to find some for you or order them for you.

And of course, you can also search for books on any topic at online bookstores. The printed books can be delivered right to your door, or ebooks can be sent electronically to your electronic reader. It's like magic!

Speaking of going online, you can find tons of information about the presidents there. You don't even have to read a book. Just go to Google or any other search engine and type in the topic you want to learn more about. Type "Presidents." Or "Weird facts about the presidents." Or "Weird facts about Abraham Lincoln." Trust me, hundreds of websites are going to come up. You might be sitting at the computer all day.

You should be careful doing online research, though, because *anybody* can put up a website and post any kind of information there, so you can't be sure if the "facts" are true. At least with a book, a fact-checker at the publishing company made sure that the author didn't just make up a bunch of stuff. Like, if Arlo said in this book that Grover Cleveland invented pajamas, the fact-checker would look it up. If he or she couldn't find proof of that, we would have to take it out of the book.

And by the way, Grover Cleveland did

not invent pajamas. Pajamas were invented in India and the Far East. Do you know how I know? I looked it up!

Now, I know you probably like to go online with your friends and search for dumb stuff like videos of cats playing the piano. But really, how many videos of cats playing piano can one kid watch? I've seen plenty of videos of cats playing pianos, and they're pretty much all the same. The first few are funny, but then it gets boring after a while.

And let me clue you in on a little secret— CATS CAN'T PLAY THE PIANO. Oh, sure, they can put their little paws on the keys and make some noises. But that's not the same as playing the piano! Why do so many kids waste so much time watching cats playing the piano? That's what I want to know.

Hey, maybe that will be my next online research project!

Anyway, what I'm trying to say is that you should stop watching dumb cat videos and look up more important stuff. You might learn something. Who knows?

Maybe you'll go to Harvard someday, like me.

Hey, maybe you and I will be in the same class at Harvard! Then we can be study buddies!

Okay, that's all I have to say. I have to go now. I need to go look stuff up on my computer. Like why kids waste so much time watching videos of cats playing the piano. But on the next few pages, there are some cool puzzles and games about the presidents. Have fun.

Bye!

Andrea

FUN GAMES AND WEIRD WORD PUZZLES

LIFE, LIBERTY, AND THE PURSUIT OF WORDS

Directions: Can you find these ten words from the story hidden in the messy jumble of letters below?

```
T E I C H A L L E N G E A T F
I N D E P E N D E N C E G L K
F X T L K U I J N Q D C E P L
V P R E S I D E N T G C D M P
Q G X C B K B B P C N X X J R
E O B A M A V L D E L E C T I
T G P W N P N I M H K O B D Z
E Z I H G B J N D D F F D X E
D K O N Y X E C N P Q Z R U R
D V E E I B R O V T A K P Z Y
Y K L D H O R L F O P Y S W D
U F H Q W S L N O I H O L I N
Y K N F F I T Q L L L Y F W D
G T I D B N E Y K E X G T A D
B I L L T Y Z Q F T R M E Y W
```

PRESIDENT CHALLENGE **PRIZE** LINCOLN **TEDDY**
INDEPENDENCE **TOILET** OBAMA **BILL** ELECT

THE PEOPLE'S CROSSWORD

Directions: Use the clues below to fill in this crossword puzzle with answers from *My Weird School: We're Red, Weird, and Blue! What Can We Do?*

ACROSS

2. The third prize for the Presidents' Day Challenge is a trip to this place.

4. Ella Mentry School's opponent.

6. The place where the sitting president lives.

7. There are eleven _____ in this book.

DOWN

1. Last name of the first president of the United States.

3. Fifty-seven people signed the Declaration of _____.

5. What Mr. Porky sells.

7. What we flip to choose who goes first in a challenge.

THE GREAT AMERICAN WORD JUMBLE

Directions: The eight words below are all jumbled up! Can you put the letters in the correct order to uncover the words from the story?

HBUTTAB: _____

VRHOOE: _____

ETSTCNO: _____

ROCCANO: _____

CUTOINTOSNIT: _____

VNIIARGI: _____

QUOITNSE: _____

SUHB: _____

FOUR SCORE AND TEN MATCHES AGO

Directions: Each of the words or phrases in the list below matches one of the words on the next page. See if you can pair them up!

Dollar → _____

Civil → _____

Winning → _____

Baskin- → _____

Media → _____

Oral → _____

Bragging → _____

Front → _____

Super → _____

A-MAZE-ING GRACE

Directions: A.J. and Andrea won a free trip to DizzyLand, the coolest place in the history of the world. Plus, they get to bring all their friends. Now help them find their way there!

WORD SUMMIT

Directions: Words can do weird things when you scramble them! See how many smaller words you can make using the letters from these bigger words and phrases. Try to come up with at least ten new, smaller words for each!

Here's an example:

MY WEIRD SCHOOL

1. Wool   2. Dire   3. Loom

Washington Monument	James Madison	Dirk School

MY WEIRD SCHOOL TRIVIA QUESTIONS

There's no way in a million hundred years you'll get all these answers right. So nah-nah-nah boo-boo on you! (Hint: all the answers to the questions below can be found in the My Weird School Special books, including this one.)

Q: WHAT MONTH DOES A.J. HATE?
A: February

Q: WHEN DID A.J. AND HIS FRIENDS FIRST COMPETE AGAINST DIRK SCHOOL?
A: During the Brain Games

Q: WHAT DOES ALEXIA USE TO GET AROUND?
A: A skateboard

Q: WHAT DOES "PRINGLE UP" MEAN?

A: To line up like Pringles

Q: WHAT TYPE OF ANIMAL DOES NEIL KEEP AS A PET?

A: A ferret

Q: WHO WAS THE FIRST PRESIDENT TO USE EMAIL?

A: Bill Clinton

Q: WHO IS THE STAR OF THE DIRK SCHOOL TV STATION?

A: Morgan Brocklebank

Q: WHAT WAS ELLA MENTRY SCHOOL'S MEDIA CENTER FORMERLY KNOWN AS?

A: The library

Q: WHO LOVES TO DRESS UP AS FAMOUS PEOPLE IN HISTORY?

A: Mrs. Roopy

Q: WHAT DOES P.A.C. STAND FOR?

A: Principal Advisory Committee

Q: WHICH GROWN-UP AT ELLA MENTRY SCHOOL IS BALD?

A: Mr. Klutz

Q: WHAT SCHOOL DOES ANDREA WANT TO ATTEND WHEN SHE'S OLDER?

A: Harvard

Q: WHAT DOES MR. COOPER DO TO MAKE EVERYONE CALM DOWN?

A: Makes a peace sign

Q: WHOSE FACE IS ON THE FIVE-THOUSAND-DOLLAR BILL?

A: James Madison

Q: WHERE DOES A.J. WANT TO MOVE TO WHENEVER HE'S EMBARRASSED?

A: Antarctica to live with the penguins

Q: WHO IS EMILY'S FAVORITE PRESIDENT?
A: Abraham Lincoln

Q: WHICH OF A.J.'S FRIENDS WILL EAT ANYTHING, EVEN IF IT ISN'T FOOD?
A: Ryan

Q: WHAT SUBJECT IS MR. COOPER USUALLY TEACHING WHEN ANNOUNCEMENTS ARE MADE?
A: Math

Q: WHO DID A.J. WRITE HIS PRESIDENTS' DAY ORAL REPORT ABOUT?
A: Benjamin Franklin

Q: WHO INVENTED THE TELEPHONE?
A: Alexander Graham Bell

ANSWER KEY

LIFE, LIBERTY, AND THE PURSUIT OF WORDS

```
T E I (C H A L L E N G E) A T F
(I N D E P E N D E N C E) G L K
F X T L K U I J N Q D C E P L
V (P R E S I D E N T) G C D M P
Q G X C B K B B P C N X X R
E (O B A M A) V L D (E L E C T) I
T G P W N P N I M H K O B D Z
E Z I H G B J N D D F F D X E
D K O N Y X E C N P Q Z R U R
D V E E I B R O V T A K P Z Y
Y K L D H O R L F O P Y S W D
U F H Q W S L N I H O L I N
Y K N F F I T Q L L L Y F W D
G T I D B N E Y K E X G T A D
(B I L L) T Y Z Q F (T) R M E Y W
```

THE PEOPLE'S CROSSWORD

```
                    W¹
  D²  I³  Z   Z   Y   L   A   N   D
  N       S
  D       H
  E       D⁴  I   R   K
  P       I
  E       N           S⁵
  N       G           A
  D   W⁶  H   I   T   E   H   O   U   S   E
  E       O           S
  N       N           A
  C                   G
  E       C⁷  H   A   P   T   E   R   S
          O           S
          I
          N
```

THE GREAT AMERICAN
WORD JUMBLE

Bathtub   Constitution

Hoover   Virginia

Contest   Question

Raccoon   Bush

FOUR SCORE AND TEN MATCHES AGO

Lightning → **round**

Dollar → **bill**

Civil → **war**

Winning → **team**

Baskin- → **Robbins**

Media → **center**

Oral → **report**

Bragging → **rights**

Front → **row**

Super → **Bowl**

A-MAZE-ING GRACE

WORD SUMMIT

Here are a few of the many words you may have found.

Washington Monument	James Madison	Dirk School
moon	jam	look
ton	mad	irk
mom	made	old
hinge	son	cord
went	sad	rid
tunes	sides	cool
gone	done	sold
hint	node	risk
tongue	seam	cod
what	dais	kid

THE WORLD OF DAN GUTMAN CHECKLIST

MY WEIRD SCHOOL

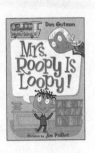

  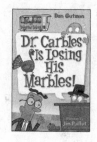

MY WEIRD SCHOOL DAZE

MY WEIRDER SCHOOL

MY WEIRD SCHOOL SPECIAL

MY WEIRDEST SCHOOL

 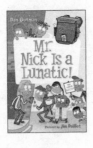  

MY WEIRDER-EST SCHOOL

MY WEIRD SCHOOL FAST FACTS

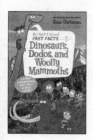

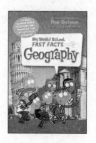

MY WEIRD TIPS

MY WEIRD SCHOOL
JOKES, GAMES, AND PUZZLES